BACK ALLEY DISCIPLINE

DOMESTIC DISCIPLINE BUNDLE

SUBMISSIVE WIVES
BOOK TWO

LEE RILEY

OLIVIA'S BACKDOOR

A DOMESTIC DISCIPLINE SPANKING ROMANCE

CHAPTER ONE

Olivia didn't know what she'd done to earn so many spankings lately. She was maintaining the house, she was available to her husband in the bedroom, and overall she was following the rules and not doing anything wrong... and yet for the past month, Paul had been bending her over almost daily.

She trusted her husband's judgment, Olivia reminded herself. She'd agreed to base their marriage on Domestic Discipline because it really did make sense; with Paul in charge of things in their relationship she not only felt loved and cherished, but was able to relax and support him without bickering over the petty things.

Paul's word was the law in their home, and when he told her it was time for punishment she accepted that he knew best. When they had first started the lifestyle about a year ago he had started out by giving her daily maintenance spankings, not because she'd done anything wrong, but simply to help her adjust.

Even though her bottom had been sore, Paul had been right. Starting every day with a good, hard spanking had helped reinforce her choice to stay submissive and humble and keep her focused on making good choices and always doing the right thing.

Domestic Discipline was a perfect fit for Olivia's compliant personality, and she'd quickly learned to anticipate Paul's needs and fall in line with his decisions. He'd had to punish her less and less, and over time the daily maintenance had faded away and been replaced with much less frequent punishment spankings that were always well deserved.

That's what made the return to daily spankings over the last month so confusing to her.

Not that Olivia minded, since she trusted that her husband always knew what she needed -- often better than she did herself. Other than daily discipline, Paul had always used every spanking as true and well deserved punishment and Olivia had learned to accept the pain, soreness, and tears that accompanied them as part of her role in the marriage.

In truth, when she went too long between spankings she started to get a little nervous, almost restless. She would started to wonder if Paul still loved her, and if she still mattered enough to him that he was paying attention to her and her needs. To her shame, she had occasionally found herself acting out if it had been a while since he'd last bent her over and paddled her. Even though she didn't enjoy it while she was bent over and taking it, a good, hard spanking always seemed to reassure her of Paul's love and settle her down.

Now he was back to spanking her every day. He hadn't told her it was maintenance, but he also hadn't told her what she'd done to deserve punishment. He seemed to bend her over whenever the whim hit him, sometimes for a few quick swats with his bare hand, but more and more lately he'd escalated to the paddle, his belt, and the horrible cane.

Olivia knew she had to trust him, but damn. Her ass was getting sore.

CHAPTER TWO

"Liv, I need you to go upstairs," Paul said as he came up behind her.

They had just finished dinner and Olivia was in the kitchen cleaning up. She'd made lasagna, his favorite, and everything had seemed fine over the meal. Paul hadn't complained about a single thing, and as he stood behind her he kissed her lightly on the neck and ran his hands up and down her sides. For a moment she wondered if he were just feeling frisky, but then he continued.

"Take off your clothes and wait for me. You've earned another spanking."

The dishes were only half done, something he usually wouldn't tolerate. It was just further proof that something was definitely out of whack. Olivia knew he didn't like her to question his authority, but this time she couldn't contain herself. Turning around in his arms she looked up at him pleadingly.

"Honey, what have I done?"

A strange look washed over Paul's face, so quickly she almost missed it. Shame? Then he lowered his brows and reprimanded her sternly.

"I didn't tell you to question me, Olivia. I told you to go get ready for what you deserve."

"Yes, sir," she answered meekly.

By the time Paul joined her in the bedroom Olivia had undressed and was waiting for him. Paul had always required her to take her spankings naked as a way to help her remember that she needed to stay humble and submissive.

In the early days of their Domestic Discipline lifestyle her nakedness has excited them both, and more often than not she'd get a healthy serving of sex along with her daily spanking. It was another thing she'd missed when he stopped disciplining her daily.

The fact that now he'd started spanking her daily but hadn't been fucking her along with it made her anxious. They still had a regular sex life, but Olivia worried that he had become too used to her. Maybe even bored.

Paul didn't say anything to her when he walked in. He barely even glanced at her. Seating himself on her vanity bench, he patted his knee and waited expectantly. Oliva hurried to him and lay herself over his lap. He was still wearing his work pants, and they scratched against her soft skin uncomfortably as he held her down.

Olivia wondered if he'd reach for her wooden hairbrush, but instead he smacked her left butt cheek with a lightly stinging blow from his bare hand. He alternated between her right and left sides for a few swats, and then pushed her legs open wider and started putting a little more power into it.

Even with the stronger smacks, Olivia could tell that he was only halfheartedly spanking her. The gentle treatment was welcome, since her bottom was bruised and still had unhealed welts on it from earlier in the week, but it still put her stomach in knots at the thought that he just didn't care anymore. Even though she knew it could earn her a much harsher punishment, she was about to speak up when he suddenly stopped.

"Stand up, Livvie," he ordered.

She did as she was told, and shifted nervously from foot to foot as he prepared a spot for her on the bed. Grabbing a few of the pillows, he piled them near the edge of the mattress until he was satisfied with the height.

"Come here and bend over the bed."

Once she did, he stood behind her without touching her for a minute, and then adjusted the pillows again and spread her legs wide. Pushing her back down with a hand between her shoulder blades, he forced her chest down and left her with her ass raised and fully exposed. She knew that with the way he'd spread her legs open her pussy was also facing him, and it was a sad reminder of earlier days when he would set her up this way and then end up fucking her before he got around to the spanking.

To Olivia's surprise, once she was in position nothing happened. She could hear Paul breathing heavily behind her, but he didn't move.

"H-honey," she asked tentatively when the silence had stretched on too long. "Are you going to spank me?"

Instead of answering, Paul stepped in close and ran his hand over her curvy bottom. He started tracing the shapes of the healing welts, and then moving up and down her thighs and finally running his hand up and down her crack. Not knowing what he was thinking was killing her, and his light touch on her sensitized flesh was starting to turn her on.

"Paul," she finally asked breathlessly. "Is-is everything okay? I've been trying to be good, and of course I'll take whatever you think I deserve, but... won't you tell me why I've been punished so much lately? So I can do better in the future?"

Olivia held her breath, half expecting to hear the whooshing sound of the cane followed by fiery slashes of pain for her impertinence. Instead, to her surprise, Paul's hands on her stilled and he apologized.

"I'm sorry, Livvie" he replied. "You've been doing very well. The problem is… me."

Olivia sucked in a breath. Her husband *never* admitted any wrongdoing. She felt tears prick behind her eyes as she jumped to the only obvious conclusion. He wasn't happy with her anymore. Desperately grasping for another answer, she pressed forward.

"Is something going wrong at work?"

"No," Paul sighed. "It's us. Me. Our marriage."

Olivia wanted to sit up and face him, but he held her down. She started crying in earnest and knew that she wasn't above begging. Paul was her world, and where he was concerned she had no shame. She would do anything if it would keep him happy.

"Please, honey, tell me what I've done," she beseeched him. "You know my role is to serve you in our marriage. If I'm failing, just tell me what you need."

"Are you sure about that?" Paul finally asked after a heavy pause.

"Anything!"

Paul started stroking her ass again, running his fingers up and down the crack between her reddened cheeks.

"Olivia, do you remember when we started Domestic Discipline, and this -- having you bent over and willing -- used to turn me on?"

Olivia cringed when she heard "used to", but nodded.

"I believe in daily maintenance," he continued. "It keeps you humble, and at first it was a great outlet for the little stresses in life. But... I had to stop. It got to the point when I felt like I was just using it as an excuse to fuck you."

"Paul, you don't need an excuse! You're my husband. You know my body is yours, whenever you need it."

Olivia's mind was reeling. Had she done something that had made Paul think she wasn't willing? She reveled in her role as his submissive wife, and if her body could service him and give him what he wanted then as far as she was concerned that was her duty. And her pleasure.

As her husband, Paul had the right to use her in whatever way he needed.

"I want to do things to you that aren't natural, Olivia," he told her quietly. "Having you bent over in front of me day after day, I can't help but look at you. I want--"

Paul's voice trailed off. The tip of his finger was resting on her tightly puckered back hole and Olivia heard his breathing quicken as he started rubbing it in firm little circles. No one had ever touched her there, and it caused unexpected shivers to shoot through her.

"I want to fuck you in the ass, Liv," he continued, his voice deepening. "I know it's not right. I know it's dirty and unclean. But every time I spank you I can't stop thinking about it. It's starting to affect my ability to discipline you properly."

His backdoor massage was starting to become more aggressive, and to her shock Olivia felt her pussy tighten with excitement. A part of her was disgusted that he would touch her in such a dirty way, but another part of her wished he would do more.

"Olivia, I-- I love your tight pussy. I love sinking into your wet heat. I love your tits and your curves and... baby, something's wrong with me. I love fucking you but, lately, nothing makes me harder than the idea of pounding my cock into your dark, dirty ass. I want to see it buried in you from behind. I want to hear you scream as I force my way into this tight little star. I want to look down and watch myself slide in and out of the most forbidden part of you."

Paul was panting, and he'd shoved his thick finger inside her ass while he ranted. Olivia gasped at the intrusion, but before she could help herself she also moaned and shoved herself toward him to force it deeper.

"I want to pound you so hard that you can't walk, until you beg me to stop, and then shoot my cum right up your backdoor," he growled.

Olivia had never heard her husband say anything so nasty. He'd always treated her with respect and care, especially during sex. Her clit was throbbing and she ground it against the pillows trying to find some satisfaction. Paul was driving his finger in and out of her ass, and the rough treatment was a mix of pleasure and pain that drove her crazy.

"Do it! Paul, *please*," she begged.

His finger stilled, and then with an oath he ripped it out of her and stripped off his clothes. Within moments, he'd replaced it with the tip of his cock. His head was slick with precum, but he didn't wait to lubricate her. He was too far gone.

Grabbing her ass with both hands, Paul pulled her open and drove himself in past her tightly clenched virgin hole. As he breached her ass for the first time, Olivia cried and tried to jerk away. His cock was much bigger than the finger that had excited her and it forced her open with a painful stretch that she wasn't sure if she could bear.

"Paul!"

He paused with just the head of his cock inside her. They both stilled, breathing heavily, until he spanked her with a stinging smack. It made her tighten around him, and he groaned in ecstasy.

"Livvie, I'm going to fuck you in the ass now, and you're just going to have to take it."

Paul pushed himself deeper inside her and Olivia's hands fisted in the bedcover as she tried to relax her tight channel around his invasion. She felt like he was splitting her in two, but she'd had a lot of experience submitting to his punishment and decided this was no different. She forced herself to be still, then whimpered as he pulled back and drove in even deeper.

Paul pumped himself in and out of her, using his hands to alternate between spanking her, kneading her round cheeks, and pulling her open even wider as he finally let himself take what he'd wanted for so long.

"You're so dirty," he panted. "You deserve to be fucked like a whore."

Olivia gasped, then moaned. She couldn't believe her husband would say such a thing, or that it had almost made her come when he did.

"*Yes!*" she cried out as he slammed himself all the way in. His cock ripped through her resistance and his hard thrusts started to push her forward on the bed. Paul growled behind her and reached out to fist his hand in the long hair that was spread across her back.

"Stay right here and take it," he ordered.

He yanked her head back and fucked her ass even harder as she panted and begged. Olivia was losing it. She'd always enjoyed sex but had never felt the desperate inflamed need that consumed her. Shoving a hand between her legs, she frantically rubbed at her clit while her husband pounded his cock into her from behind.

"Oh, God! Oh, Paul! Oh, *Fuck!*"

Olivia came so hard that she almost bent in two. Her ass clenched around Paul's cock as the waves of her orgasm pulsed through her. He was buried to the hilt as she milked him with her ass, and as soon as her hole loosened enough for him to move he pulled back and slammed into her, again and again, until he came.

Gasping, he shot his load deep into the steamy depths of her ass. Paul collapsed on top of his wife as his body shuddered and stilled.

Neither one of them moved for a long minute.

Finally, Paul stirred. His softening cock was still buried inside Olivia, and he wrapped his arms around her and rolled them both onto their sides so he could stay put. Kissing her sweaty neck softly, he tried to catch his breath.

"Paul," she finally asked. "Will you--"

"Will I what, Liv?"

"Will you fuck me like that every day?" she whispered, blushing.

"You liked it in the ass?"

Olivia nodded. She knew it was nasty, but she also knew that she wouldn't be able to give it up now that she'd had a taste. Paul's cock started to swell inside her, and she sucked in a breath.

"Oh *yes*. Please," she begged.

Paul started to rock his hips behind her as his erection grew. Her body hummed with excitement, and Olivia smiled in anticipation.

She was so glad she'd trusted her husband. He always knew just what she needed.

SOPHIE'S PUNISHMENT

A DOMESTIC DISCIPLINE SPANKING ROMANCE

CHAPTER ONE

Sophie glanced at the clock, then looked back at the dirty dishes in the sink and sighed. Her husband, Luke, should be home within the hour and there was no way she was going to get the house in shape before he arrived.

Luke had been out of town for a week, and Sophie was going stir crazy. The couple lived a Domestic Discipline lifestyle, and Sophie was used to getting daily maintenance spankings every morning in addition to the punishment spankings Luke delivered as the Head of their Household whenever she broke the rules.

Like not keeping the house clean.

Her attitude and habits had really slipped without her husband home to reinforce them over the past week.

All day Sophie had been glancing at the clock, counting down the hours until he would finally be home. And all day she'd found one way or another to procrastinate cleaning up.

She knew she needed a spanking to clear her head and calm her heart. Why couldn't she just *ask* him for one, she thought to herself in disgust. She didn't need to play this game of breaking the house rules... sure, she'd get the spanking she needed, but it was at the expense of his happiness, and at the expense of the orderly house he expected to come home to.

Thinking of how hard Luke worked to keep their family in the style they were accustomed to, Sophie was suddenly filled with shame to think she would consider making his life harder just to selfishly meet her own needs. Suddenly determined to get everything done before he walked in the door, she became a whirlwind of activity as she raced from room to room putting the house to rights.

Too late.

Sophie froze as the sound of the front door opening told her that her husband had come home early. She was torn between her eagerness to see him and her embarrassment that he was returning to the mess she'd let accumulate in his absence.

"Sophie," Luke said in a tired voice behind her.

Turning, she jumped up and wrapped herself around him with a happy squeal. Covering his face with kisses, all her concerns were temporarily forgotten as she basked in the feeling of Luke's strong arms around her.

After several happy minutes, he laughingly peeled her off of him and set her down.

"I'm exhausted, sugar," he told her. "Would you please make me a quick bite in the kitchen, and then unpack my suitcase so we can go straight to bed?"

"Yes, sir," Sophie replied happily. She was already feeling calmer now that he was home.

As he headed upstairs to take a shower Sophie went into the kitchen and put together a plate of food for her man. Setting him a place at the table, she rushed back in to try to put the kitchen right. She was at the sink, and when he walked in behind her she heard Luke's heavy sigh of disappointment.

"You really let it go, didn't you, Sophie?"

She turned to him, subdued. It was one thing to crave his authority while he was away, but now that he was back and so obviously exhausted, she was filled with shame for putting this added burden on him.

"I am really, really tired tonight, and the last thing I wanted to have to do was take time to punish you," he sat down heavily and began to eat. "Having me out of town doesn't mean you don't need to follow the rules."

"I know that, sir," Sophie said quietly. "I'm so sorry."

"Go up to the room and take off your clothes. You'll be in corner time until I finish eating, and then we'll get to your spanking."

Sophie did as she was told. Once she had taken off her clothes, she went straight to the corner of their bedroom that Luke had designated for her discipline. She stood facing the wall, elbows bent and fingers laced together on top of her head.

The room was cool, as she had opened the bedroom window earlier in anticipation of her husband's return. He couldn't stand sleeping in a hot room. As she waited, the night breeze made her shiver, and her nipples hardened with the cold. She knew she was supposed to use this time to think about her behavior, but she found herself getting aroused instead.

Sophie didn't enjoy the pain of her punishments, of course, but Luke always allowed her to give him a formal thank you afterward. The thought of falling to her knees and having his cock in her mouth again after a whole week without him made her clench her thighs together as her pussy started to tingle.

She was so focused on her passionate thoughts that she didn't hear Luke come up behind her. When he ran his hand down her naked back and over her smooth ass, she jumped. He sighed with displeasure.

"Sugar, I would much rather have come home and fucked you than had to spank you. Please remember that your failure to follow the rules while I was gone has made this harder on both of us."

She squirmed at his words. She felt guilty for the extra strain she had caused him, but his words just made her hornier.

Luke brought her over to the bed and bent her over his knee. With one hand, he reached under her and held the firm weight of her dangling right breast. Kneading it and pinching the nipple, he brought his other hand down in a hard smack on her bare ass. Sophie moaned as excitement made her throb.

With hard, stinging slaps he alternated between her left and right cheeks until they were cherry red. She knew he must be exhausted, because he didn't stop working on her sensitive nipple the whole time. Normally, Luke was very strict about not letting her get too turned on during discipline, but tonight he seemed oblivious to what he was doing to her as he let himself enjoy her body. As his blows got harder, she felt his thick cock start to swell under her.

Stopping suddenly, he removed his hand and sat breathing heavily while his dick twitched against her.

"Sophie, your punishment isn't over, but I think we both realize you're enjoying this too much. And it's distracting me, too. Get on your knees and thank me before we continue," he told her.

Happily complying, she slid off his lap and pulled his thick cock out of his pants. Unable to wait, she bent closer to suck on each of his balls before licking her way up the hard shaft and wrapping her lips around the bulging head.

"Suck it hard, sugar," her husband ordered. "I need to be able to focus for the rest of your spanking and I want you to make me come, fast."

Holding his balls in one hand, she held his cock steady and pumped her head up and down over the throbbing length. Her cheeks started aching immediately, reminding her of how long it had been since she'd had him in her mouth. Relaxing her throat as he'd taught her, she sucked him in and out hard and deep, making his balls slap against her chin.

Luke normally liked to take charge, fisting his hands in her hair to hold her steady and pounding himself down her throat until he came. Tonight, though, he was so tired that he let Sophie do all the work.

When she had him deep in her throat she swallowed around his straining cock, massaging it again and again with her throat as she forced herself to breathe through her nose. She knew he wanted to come quickly, and it worked. With a tired groan, he finally grabbed her head and held it still, pumping warm streams of cum down her throat.

"Thank you, sir," she said formally when he pulled his wet flesh out of her mouth. She used the back of her hand to wipe off her face, and then sat back on her heels waiting to hear what he wanted from her next.

"Go to the corner, sugar, and wait for me until I'm ready to finish your spanking."

Once she was there, she couldn't help wiggling her hips at him. She knew that her husband loved her firm, round ass, and when it was glowing red and hot from his discipline, he usually couldn't resist it. She was so horny that she didn't know how she would make it through without touching herself, but she knew from past punishments that she wasn't allowed to move during corner time.

She heard him open the closet where he kept the spanking implements, and shivered in nervous anticipation of what he would choose. The pain was usually enough to keep her from getting too aroused by his ministrations, but tonight she truly didn't know whether it would be enough to distract her.

Hoping his back was turned, she dared to dart a hand down and furiously rub at her clit for a moment. It was too much. She moaned as pleasure shot through her.

"Sophie!" he said sharply. "Are you breaking the rules? *Again?*"

"Yes, sir," she said breathlessly as she quickly got back into position. "I'm sorry sir."

"That's going to earn you something extra. Take one step back from the wall, sugar. I want you to spread your legs apart and bend over with your hands on the floor in front of you. Keep your legs straight. I want your ass up high. Your corner time is not over, but you will stay still until I'm ready for you to move. Is that understood?"

"Yes, sir."

He had never put her in this position before, and she waited anxiously to see what he had planned. Without any warning, she heard the tell tale hiss as he swung the dreaded rattan cane through the air. In her new position, he had easy access to the full roundness of her bottom, and she couldn't clench her buttocks to minimize any of the impact.

With unerring aim he laid into her with six fast, heavy strokes, forcing a scream out of her that turned into an extended sobbing wail. Each slice felt like a knife edge of fire that blotted out every other sensation. The afterglow of each stroke was immediately eclipsed by the streak of pain from the next.

When he finally paused, she was panting. Her ass felt heavy and hot with the memory of his strokes, and Sophie realized that it had only made her pussy wetter.

Suddenly, she felt a cool, hard pressure against her yearning cunt and realized that he was using her own juices to lubricate something. She figured out what it was a moment before he inserted it.

Her silver, diamond shaped butt plug with the word "OBEY" printed on the flange.

Luke didn't bother working it in slowly, and his sudden hard push into her anus made her gasp, and then moan. Luckily she had offered plenty of lubrication, and she clenched her hole around it to release little spurts of pleasure. There was no way that Luke didn't see how turned on she was, despite the escalating force of his punishments.

He still hadn't said a word, and with a sharp crack he resumed spanking her with a heavy, wooden paddle. The fiery pain as he spanked each check and the crease at the top of her thighs mingled with the intense pleasure that radiated from the plug each time a blow forced her to tense up.

Tears ran down her face as she felt herself getting closer and closer to climax. As if he could read her mind, Luke barked an order at her as he continued his steady rhythm with the paddle.

"Don't come!"

Sophie started crying in earnest at his command. She knew she had to obey, but she was so close that holding back was as painful as the punishment she was taking from the paddle.

"Please, sir," she begged hoarsely. "Please let me--"

"Get down on your hands and knees," he cut her off.

As soon as she was in position, she heard the paddle hit the floor and felt his hands grip her burning ass tightly. Spanking her had made his cock hard again, and she happily pressed back against him when she felt him start to push himself inside her dripping cunt.

"You're punishment isn't over, sugar," he told her as he thrust into her with a groan. "But the rest of your spanking is going to have to wait until I make you come."

The sounds of pleasure he made as he drove himself into her were enough to send her over the edge. The added pressure of her butt plug made her sheath even tighter around his thick cock. She came immediately, and the pulsing waves of her orgasm drove him into a frenzy. Pounding into her red, fiery ass he came again with a shout.

"Bend over the bed and wait for the rest of your punishment, Sophie," he directed her. "I'm going to shower and finish getting ready for bed. You are not to move or remove your plug, and I'll finish with the paddle and 20 more strokes of the cane when I'm done."

Crawling over to the bed to wait, happy tears leaked out of the corners of her closed eyes. She had needed this so much. Her heart filled with a warm glow as she thought of all that her husband did for her. As tired as he was, he had taken the time to fuck her when she needed it, and was still committed to giving her a truly severe punishment.

She knew the cane had broken her skin, and hesitantly reached back to touch her thighs. Her fingers came back pink, sticky with a combination of blood and Luke's cum as it leaked out of her. Now that he was home, she would be able to toe the line and benefit from his daily discipline. She sighed in contentment at the thought of how much better things always were when he was there.

CHAPTER TWO

The next morning, Sophie woke up to waves of pain in her lower body. After finishing her punishment the night before, Luke had told her to unpack his suitcase, wash the laundry he'd brought back with him, and clean herself up before coming to bed.

She'd finished just after midnight, and obeying his directive to leave the plug in her anus until further notice, she'd crawled in next to him and cuddled into his warmth. When she woke up, he had a heavy arm flung over her and his morning hard on was putting pressure on her plug as he sleepily ground against her from behind.

As happy as the feeling of his morning arousal always made her, having him rub himself against her bruised, raw flesh made her hiss in pain.

"Good morning, sugar," Luke whispered in his ear as he lifted the blankets and pushed down on her shoulders. "I need your lips around my cock this morning."

Wiggling herself down between his legs, she licked and sucked him as he lay relaxed on the bed. It was the second time that he'd let her do all the work, and she was determined to make him happy. She could tell he was enjoying having her service him, but before she could finish him off, Luke suddenly pushed her off of his cock and pulled her back up against him.

With her breasts flattened against his broad chest, he ran his hands down her back to cup her raw ass and play with her plug. The instant pleasure/pain had her clutching his shoulders and hoping he would let her come before her morning maintenance spanking.

Turning her over, he pushed her face down onto the bed and told her to get her knees up. Lifting her red ass to his view, he held her shoulders down against the bed while he slowly pulled the plug out with his other hand.

"I'm going to fuck you in the ass, sugar," he told her. "And then I'm going to take a shower while you make me breakfast."

"B-but, sir," she said plaintively as she felt his wet cock press into her back hole. "What about my maintenance spanking?"

"After breakfast," he promised with a smile in his voice. "You are such a spanking slut. Now let me hear how much you like what I'm giving you."

Pushing into her from behind, he buried himself to the hilt. He hadn't used her this way before and she was thankful he'd left the plug in overnight to get her ready. She was stretched enough that the way he filled her felt amazing. Before long, the friction from his pounding thrusts had her panting with excitement, and she did as she'd been told, moaning and thanking him as he fucked her ass.

When he finally came, she squirmed in silent frustration. She was still turned on and hadn't had any release. Luke chuckled as he swatted her ass and headed to the shower.

"Don't you touch yourself, sugar," he warned as he closed the bathroom door.

Pouting, Sophie grabbed her robe and headed downstairs to get his breakfast ready. Restlessly moving around the kitchen, she paused to wipe the cum leaking from behind her on a kitchen towel. Knowing she shouldn't, she furtively started to finger herself while her hand was down there.

Even as she did it, she couldn't believe she was breaking the rules *again*. Tossing the towel aside, she went back to making Luke's breakfast. She threw some bacon and eggs on the stove and pulled out the hand mixer to start his biscuits. Turning it on, she felt the humming vibration of the little tool travel up her arm, and it was just too much.

Sophie turned it off and pulled the mixing blades out of the appliance quickly. Thrusting it under her robe, she squeezed it between her legs and turned it back on. Riding it hard, she forgot to listen for the sound of the shower going off as she used the little kitchen tool's vibration to make herself come.

As soon as she did, she felt a heavy hand on her shoulder. Uh oh.

"Sophie," Luke said said with a little smile and a shake of his head. "What am I going to do with you?"

"Spank me?" she asked hopefully. Then sighed happily when he took her hand and led her back upstairs.

LEXI'S FIRST SPANKING

A DOMESTIC DISCIPLINE SPANKING
ROMANCE

CHAPTER ONE

Lexi had butterflies in her stomach as she started to unbutton her shirt. She and Josh had waited to sleep with each other until they were married, and after just two weeks, the act of undressing in front of him was still new enough to make her blush.

She trusted her new husband completely. Even though she was nervous about this new idea of his she was willing to at least give it a try.

Lexi hadn't been spanked since she was a little girl, and when Josh had first sat her down to talk to her about Domestic Discipline she'd immediately had flashbacks to the punishment her stern father had dealt out whenever she'd earned it. She would be the first to agree that spanking had definitely worked. Lexi had become a very good girl.

The thought of bending over her husband's knee right now was making her palms sweat and doing strange things to her stomach. Not altogether bad things.

"You want to... *punish* me?" she'd asked in surprise when he'd first brought it up.

"No, baby, it's not like that. It's a whole lifestyle," Josh had explained. "Spankings and punishment are part of it, for sure, but mostly it's a way for me to take care of you like I want to. To make sure that you always feel loved and protected."

Josh had been the most attentive man Lexi had ever dated, and her heart warmed as he went on to explain how he'd come across the idea while searching for ways to be a good husband. She'd never felt as cherished and cared for as she did with Josh, and the fact that she got to spend a lifetime with this man still left her breathless.

"Okay," she'd finally agreed. "We can give it a try, if you think it's best."

That first conversation had happened just a few days after their wedding, right after they'd made love. They'd been naked and entwined with each other in bed, and Lexi had felt her husband's cock start to swell again upon her agreement. His rising excitement had sent a little thrill of anticipation through her. She still wasn't used to how active their sex life had become.

Lexi was 23, and she hadn't been a virgin when she and Josh first met. It had surprised her that he wanted to wait until marriage to have sex. Even though she'd appreciated his traditional values and the way he treated her so respectfully, a tiny part of her had been impatient to find out what their sex life would be like.

Not that her previous sexual experiences had been very exciting. Lexi had lost her virginity at 19. She'd wanted to wait until she was truly in love, and the guy she'd finally given it to had sworn up and down that he felt the same.

The sex, though, had been a disappointment, and Lexi's heart had been truly shattered when she'd found out that her first lover hadn't been sincere. Once he'd finally gotten in her pants he'd quickly lost interest, and the whole thing had left her feeling pretty wary of jumping into bed with anyone else.

It had been a couple of years before she gave sex another try. She'd known from the start that she didn't really love guy number two. At 21, she'd simply decided that it didn't matter. Good girl or not, she'd wanted to find out what all the fuss was about sex. Lexi was healthy and horny and willing to experiment.

Unfortunately, her second lover was just as unsatisfying as the first one. Neither man had bothered to bring her to orgasm, and she'd come to the conclusion that maybe she just wasn't any good at it.

Which had just made it all the easier to wait when Josh asked her. Secretly, she worried that he'd be disappointed in her when they finally consummated their marriage and she'd been beyond nervous on her wedding night. Maybe even more so than if she'd come to him a virgin.

Josh had undressed her slowly, almost reverently, and for some reason that had made her expect the same treatment in bed. Instead, as soon as she was naked in front of him, he'd forcefully pushed her down on her knees. Unzipping his slacks, he'd pulled out his erection and rubbed the tip across her lips.

"Baby, I want you to suck me off before I fuck you for the first time," he'd said in a loving voice that was strangely at odds with his crude language. "I've been waiting for you for so long, I don't think I'll last unless I come down your throat, first."

Lexi had frozen with disbelief. This wasn't what she'd expected from him. Josh had always treated her with kid gloves, but now he held her down firmly with one hand on top of her head while the other relentlessly pressed his thick cock against her closed lips.

She'd never given a blow job before, but he wasn't giving her much choice. A hot tingle shot between her legs at the thought. She knew it was her husband's right to claim her, she'd just never expected to have him do it so forcefully.

Or that she would like it.

She opened her lips and he slid his cock inside her hot mouth with a groan. The salty sweet taste of his precum was new, and she rolled her tongue around his shaft as he pushed himself deeper.

"That's right, Lexi," he praised her as he moved both hands to her head to guide her. "Now suck."

Lexi did as she was told, and before long she found a rhythm that had her husband panting. He started to fuck her mouth more forcefully, and she gripped his thighs for balance as his thrusts started to make her gag and choke.

"*Fuck*, baby," Josh gritted out as his cock started to swell in her mouth. "Suck me harder! I'm going to come, and I want you to swallow all of it."

Lexi's cheeks started to ache with the unfamiliar work, but his excitement was turning her on so much that she didn't care. She sucked him as hard and deep as she could, pulling him to the very back of her throat as he slammed himself into her one last time. He came with a shout, and Lexi's wet pussy throbbed with need as he pumped warm shots of cum into her mouth.

Josh had pulled her up as soon as she'd swallowed it and given her a bruising kiss before pushing her onto her back on the bed. She'd expected him to be gentle, but the dominating way he took physical control of her already had her more aroused than she'd ever been with the two other men she'd slept with.

"I want to see you touch yourself," her husband said.

Lexi immediately blushed. Josh was still fully dressed, and she wanted to squirm and cover herself as she lay before him.

"Don't," he said sternly when she started to do just that. "Put your hands on your breasts."

Tentatively, she cupped her sensitive breasts. As Josh watched, she rubbed her fingers over her nipples and then pinched them. Hard.

She moaned, embarrassing herself.

"That's right, baby" Josh encouraged her. "Now I want to see you rub your clit."

Lexi slid a hand over her taut stomach and found her aching nub. Her hips involuntarily arched up against her hand, and she gave a little gasp. Josh had undressed while she played with herself, and now that he was finally naked he climbed up on the bed and kneeled between her open legs.

"Faster," he ordered.

His eyes were glued to her slick slit as she rubbed and fingered herself in front of him. Even though he'd just come, Josh's cock was already growing hard again as he watched her show. He started to stroke himself with one hand and reached the other one toward her hot sex.

"I want you to come," he told her, pushing a finger deep into her tight cunt.

"Oh!"

Josh started to finger fuck her in the same rhythm he was using on his own cock. The coiling tension inside her made Lexi lose all her inhibitions, and she pressed herself against his finger in a desperate frenzy as her suddenly orgasm rocked through her.

Before the pulsing waves of her release had stopped, Josh replaced his finger with his cock and drove it into her with a hard thrust that pushed her backward on the bed.

"Fuck, Lexi," he panted as he pulled out and then forced his way in again. "That was *hot.*"

Josh had a huge cock, and she was slick and as tight as a virgin. As soon as he got her open enough he started to pound into her, hard and fast. The furious invasion was going to leave her sore, but at the moment she didn't care. His thrusts were hitting something inside her that made her want to scream and claw at his back for more. Lexi had never felt anything like this before, and when her second orgasm took her she screamed and arched up against him.

Her husband had made her come three more times before he'd finally given in to his own release that first time, and in the two weeks since then she'd spent most of her married life on her back or her knees. She readily submitted to his every demand and enjoyed every minute that he fucked her.

But this... this was different.

As Lexi set her shirt on top of the dresser and unhooked her bra, she wondered what it would be like to be spanked again. She hadn't done anything to deserve it, and a small part of her resented the idea that she was going to be punished for no reason.

Once she'd agreed to try the Domestic Discipline lifestyle Josh had explained that they would start with daily maintenance spankings to keep her focused on good behavior.

The spankings she remembered from her childhood had *hurt*. She remembered the feeling of dread each time her father had sat down and patted his knee with that look. *Alexandra*, he'd say. *You've done wrong, and because I love you I'm going to punish you to help you do better next time.*

Spankings were always done on a bare bottom, sometimes with her father's hand and sometimes with his leather belt. They were never over until she was red-faced and crying, with a sore bottom that ensured she didn't forget about what she'd done for a few days.

Maybe her husband was right. Spanking definitely kept her focused on being good.

Spankings had become less and less frequent as she became better behaved, and in a strange way, she'd started to miss them. As painful as they were, there was a raw satisfaction to the physical release of balling her eyes out on the lap of someone who loved her.

"Have you ever, um, spanked anyone, honey?" she asked her husband tentatively as she finished undressing.

"No," Josh answered in a thick voice.

He hadn't fucked her in hours, and she could see that the sight of her naked was making him regret that sex wasn't the reason she'd undressed.

Josh was seated on the edge of their bed wearing shorts and a t-shirt. He'd told her that she would get her daily spankings naked to help her remember her place. But as he waited for her to come and bend over his lap for her first spanking she could see his cock start to swell.

The sight immediately made her pussy wet, and she squeezed her thighs together tightly as her dread about the spanking was forgotten.

Lexi lipped her lips and stepped in front of him.

"Do you want me to--"

"Yes."

He yanked her down to her knees as he pulled out his rock hard cock. Lexi had become very good at giving head, and she dove down onto the straining shaft greedily. With two weeks of constant practice, she'd learned to relax her throat enough that she could now take all of him.

She licked and sucked him hungrily as Josh fisted his hands in her hair and spread his legs wider to give her full access. Lexi worked his cock deeper and deeper into her throat with each bob of her head, until she finally swallowed all of him and felt his balls press against her chin.

She started to hum just like he liked, swallowing again and again to massage his aching cock with her tight throat muscles. Josh pulled her by the hair and thrust his hips against her face as she drove him over the edge.

"Fuck! Lexi! I'm coming!"

His cum shot straight down her gut, and she smiled around his thick shaft as he emptied himself into her. She'd come to love the taste of him, and it never failed to turn her on.

Lexi had gotten so involved in sucking him off that she'd totally forgotten about getting spanked. So when he pulled her up for a quick kiss and then bent her over his lap, she let out a little squeal of surprise.

His hand came down on her bare ass without warning.

Smack!

"Oooooh!" she gasped.

As forceful as Josh was in the bedroom, he'd never hit her before. The hot sting of his bare hand when she was so aroused was intoxicating, and she instinctively arched her bottom up toward him.

"Again," she panted. "Please."

Smack!

The hot sting on her other cheek was a little harder, and Lexi moaned and spread her legs apart.

"More."

Josh spanked her rhythmically, alternating between her warm butt cheeks and the sensitive tops of her thighs. Before long her ass felt like it was on fire, and she'd wantonly spread her legs as wide as she could while he held her on his lap.

Every few smacks, Josh would aim directly for her wet pussy. The sharp whacks against her swollen flesh were unbearably erotic, and combined with the familiar pain she remembered from her childhood it was overwhelming.

Josh had held himself back when he started disciplining her, but as Lexi started moaning and grinding against him he found himself hitting her harder and harder. The smooth curves of her tight little ass were bright red, and the pink folds of her sex were dripping with musky juice.

"Harder," Lexi begged.

Josh had a raging hard on as he continued spanking her. He'd wanted to start out slowly to see how they both adjusted to the reality of him disciplining her, but now that he'd experienced the rush of smacking her hot flesh he wished he had something harder -- a belt, a paddle, anything to escalate the moment.

"Fuck, Lexi," he panted right along with her. "You're not supposed to be enjoying this."

Josh couldn't stand it anymore. He jerked her upright and pulled her to him for a punishing kiss. Her face was red from hanging over his knee for so long, and her face was streaked with tears from his stinging smacks. He ground his teeth into her lips and thrust his tongue down her throat as she crawled all over him, horny as hell.

"Please, Josh," she blurted out as he trailed hot kisses down her neck. "Fuck me, I can't stand it!"

With a growl, he stood up and flipped her onto the bed.

"Get on all fours," he ordered.

She scrambled to obey, presenting her swollen ass to him and spreading her knees wide without being told. Josh grabbed her hips and pulled her back toward the edge of the bed so that he could fuck her where he was standing.

He spanked her, hard, and then drove his cock in to the hilt. Fucking her hard and fast, he spanked and thrust until Lexi exploded. Josh held himself still while she pulsed around his aching cock, then slowly pulled his still hard shaft out of his wife.

"Don't move."

Lexi collapsed onto her elbows and lay panting. Josh had given her her very first orgasm on their wedding night, and had made her come countless times since, but she'd never been rocked by anything like what she'd just experienced.

The feel of him spanking her while he fucked her was hotter than anything she'd ever dreamt of, and she was so caught up in the aftershock that she didn't stop to wonder what else he had in store for her until she felt his finger slide over her juicy slit and continue up to her ass.

His finger was slick with her moisture, and he rubbed it in tight circles around her fully exposed ass hole. Lexi sucked in a sharp breath and tried to pull away.

"Josh, no!"

He smacked her across her throbbing ass.

"Lexi, yes," he said sternly. "I am your husband, don't ever tell me no again."

He was right, but Lexi hadn't expected him to want to use her this way. It felt wrong, and dirty. She trembled as breached her tightly clenched hole with his thick finger.

"It will go easier if you relax, baby," he said in a desire thickened voice as he started to force his finger in and out of her puckered entrance.

"It-it hurts."

Tears sprung to her eyes, and she heard his breathing quicken as he continued to work his finger inside her. She suddenly felt even more pressure as he forced a second one in.

"Please, no" she begged as he pushed her shoulders down flat on the bed and continued to fuck her hole with his fingers.

"Spanking you obviously doesn't work as a punishment, Lex," he panted behind her. "But this just might."

He forced a third finger into her and she muffled a cry against the bedspread. Her tight little ass already throbbed from the hard spanking, and now her husband's rough invasion stretched her past the point that she thought she could bear it. He started scissoring his fingers inside her, and she groaned at the aching pressure.

"I'm going to fuck you in the ass now, baby," he warned when he couldn't wait anymore.

His fingers slid out of her throbbing passage, and were instantly replaced with the thick head of his penis. He started to push it in slowly, and the relentless pressure stretched her even farther than his fingers had.

"Josh!" she cried out in pain.

Smack!

"I told you not to move, Lexi," he warned her as he continued his advance.

She felt like she was being ripped in two, and when he pulled back and thrust forward again she realized that the first time he'd only managed to get in the first few inches of his cock. Every thrust forced her open further, and he drove himself steadily deeper and deeper until he was finally able to get his full length inside her dark channel.

Lexi was panting, her entire body covered in sweat, as she tried to accept the painful stretch inside her. Josh slowly pulled back and spanked her again before thrusting in just as deeply. He continued to spank and thrust in a slow, steady rhythm that began to create a throbbing tension inside her.

"Oh!" Lexi gasped as one of his thrusts caused her pussy to throb. *"Josh!"*

It happened again. With a moan, Lexi started to push back against him. She knew it was wrong to enjoy him taking her this way, but as he started to pound into her faster and faster she realized that the dirty act was going to make her come again.

Her husband started driving into her like a jackhammer, and Lexi strained against him, begging him to fuck her in the ass even harder.

Josh had never sodomized anyone before, but he hadn't been able to resist when her forbidden hole was so sweetly presented between her red, swollen ass cheeks. As he drove his wife into a frenzy, he felt his own orgasm rising like a relentless tidal wave that threatened to swamp him with its intensity.

"Oh, God! Oh, Fuck! *Josh!*"

Josh felt Lexi's body clench around his pulsing cock at the exact same moment that he finally unloaded into her ass. He pulled her tightly against him as he pumped his seed into her from behind. The sight of his thick cock disappearing between her cheeks was the hottest thing he'd ever seen.

"You weren't supposed to enjoy your discipline, baby," he repeated what he'd said to her earlier when he finally caught his breath. He pulled out and collapsed on the bed next to his wife, pulling her against him and nuzzling her neck from behind.

"Sorry," she replied cheekily. His cum was leaking out of her stretched ass, and she wiggled her sore bottom against his soft cock. "I guess that's just one more thing you'll have to punish me for."

He growled and rolled on top of her. He was already getting hard again as he thought about her next spanking.

This Domestic Discipline thing was definitely going to work out for them.

ASHLEE'S DEGRADATION

A DOMESTIC DISCIPLINE SPANKING ROMANCE

CHAPTER ONE

When Ashlee had made her marriage vows to John "until death did they part", she had meant it. She looked down at the divorce paperwork in her hand and felt tears well up. They had only been married two years, and already this is what it had come to.

The first year of their marriage had been blissful. John was everything she'd ever wanted in a man: sexy, attentive, and commanding. He had told her that she was perfect for him in every way, from her petite curviness to her willing compliance in and out of the bedroom.

The last year, though, had started to get rocky.

On Ashlee's side of the relationship nothing had changed, but ever since John started working under his new sales manager his attitude toward her had started to shift. Ashlee knew it was uncharitable to blame her marital problems on John's work, but she had become convinced that it was true.

From the beginning, John had been the one to wear the pants in their relationship. Ashlee had blossomed under his strong hand. Lord knows *she* had no desire to run things, and having John make decisions for them both made her feel cared for and loved.

But over the last year he'd moved from authoritative to outright demanding, expecting instant obedience and showing his temper when she didn't immediately comply with something he'd ordered. Ashlee *wanted* to make him happy, but as time went on it felt like nothing she did satisfied him.

One day, John made a comment about how good his new sales manager, Aiden, had it. *His* wife was completely submissive, and always did what Aiden told her. Ashlee had been livid. He was comparing wives with his *boss?*

They had fought about it for a week, and John had finally apologized and even mellowed out for a few days. Slowly, though, he'd started dropping references to Aiden into their conversation again. Ashlee started to get sick of hearing "Aiden says this" and "Aiden thinks that"... and the one that brought on the next fight: "Mila would never...".

What? She'd demanded. *Who the fuck is Mila?*

Oh. Of course. Aiden's perfect wife who does everything he says. Ashlee had never met her, but she started to hate the bitch. Apparently Mila set the standard that her own husband was now holding her to, and every single time Ashlee failed to measure up in John's eyes.

Ashlee had been at her wit's end, and a few days ago they'd had their worst fight, ever. It had ended with Ashlee telling him to leave if he wasn't happy with her. She was shocked and heart broken when he actually did.

She hadn't heard from him since. Until this. A stranger in a suit had knocked on the door and handed her a manilla envelope after confirming her identity. Getting served with divorce papers was like a punch in the gut. She just couldn't believe her perfect marriage had fallen apart so quickly, and over something she didn't really understand.

The paperwork was starting to become damp as her tears leaked onto it. She didn't know how long she'd been sitting at the kitchen table before something snapped inside her. Fuck this. She may have promised to love, honor, and *obey* her man but she wasn't going to obey him in *this.*

Ashlee was going to fight for her marriage, and she knew just where to start.

CHAPTER TWO

"**Y**es?"

Ashlee's heart sank when she got her first look at the woman who answered the door. *Mila.* She was gorgeous, and she seemed to radiate some kind of zen calm that immediately fit with all of John's comments about how submissive and obedient she was. Ashlee couldn't imagine this woman ever back talking her husband.

"Can I help you?" Mila asked after a beat of silence.

"I'm-I'm Ashlee. John's wife."

"Who?"

Mila's look of confusion changed to one of concern as Ashlee's face crumpled into tears. Reaching out a comforting hand, Mila pulled her inside and brought her back to the kitchen. Of course it was perfect. Clean and sparkling and cute as a button, with fresh baked scones cooling on a rack and hot coffee percolating.

Ashlee looked around in despair as she tried to compose herself. She would never be able to compete with this. Mila slid a perfect cup of coffee in front of her and sat down.

"I'm sorry, Ashlee, is it? I'm not sure who you are," she said apologetically.

"My husband, John, works for Aiden."

A strange look flashed across Mila's face, but it was gone so quickly that Ashlee wasn't sure what she'd seen. Guilt? Shame?

"H-he served me with divorce papers this morning! We had a great marriage until--"

Mila patted Ashlee's arm and handed her a tissue while she cried. Finally getting control of herself, Ashlee continued.

"Until he started working for your husband. I'm sorry. I know we don't know each other, but it seems like all John's done lately is compare me to you, and find me lacking."

Mila tipped her head to the side, looking thoughtfully at the other woman while she took a sip of her own coffee. She seemed to be weighing what to say, and finally set her cup down with a decisive thunk.

"Ashlee, do you and your husband practice Domestic Discipline?"

Ashlee looked at her in confusion.

"No, um, I don't know what that is."

"In my marriage, Aiden and I have agreed that he is the Head of our Household. I love having him in charge, and I know my role in the relationship," she paused to see how Ashlee was reacting. So far so good.

"Aiden sets the rules, and I follow them. I don't question them, I just trust that he knows best. And if I fail to remember my place... there are consequences."

"Consequences? Like, what?"

Mila blushed, but kept her eyes on Ashlee's.

"He punishes me. Spanks me. Whips me. Ties me up and uses... other methods... to remind me of the rules and help me learn to obey him more completely."

"Seriously?"

Mila nodded, then surprised Ashlee by standing up and pulling her skirt up to her waist. Mila wasn't wearing any panties, and the site of her smoothly shaven pussy suddenly appearing over coffee and scones startled Ashlee so much that she gasped.

Mila turned around and exposed her pale, curvy ass. It was crisscrossed with red welts and bruises, and the sight did strange things to Ashlee's insides. It was horrible, but at the same time...

"Wha-- Um, okay. Your husband *did* that to you?"

Mila sat back down and nodded with a contented smile.

"That and more. And if you want to know the truth, I like it. Having him take ownership of my body like that, well, it's a huge turn on."

Ashlee wanted to disagree, but she couldn't. She'd had to squeeze her thighs together at the sight of Mila's ass. Seeing the marks on the other woman's perfect body had sent a rush of wet heat straight to her pussy.

"But... doesn't it hurt?"

"Well, yes, but-- I don't know how to explain it. It's like it doesn't matter. I mean, I don't like the feeling in the moment that it's happening, but I love being dominated by Aiden and being, um, *used...* in whatever way he decides is best.

It's done amazing things for our marriage, and if you've come looking for advice that's the best I can give you. Let your husband know that you're *his*, completely. Let him do whatever he needs to, to prove to himself that he truly owns you.

Trust me, if you're the kind of woman I think you are you'll end up thanking me."

CHAPTER THREE

Ashlee was waiting for John in their bedroom. She couldn't quite believe she was doing this, but she had to admit that a part of her was a little bit thrilled.

She'd stayed at Mila's house for a full hour, listening to the sexy, submissive woman describe the type of punishment and discipline that her husband used with her, and even showing Ashlee some of the equipment that they used.

Mila had helped her come up with a plan. After getting approval from her husband, she'd agreed to loan Ashlee the things she would need and then had followed her home. She'd supervised Ashlee as she showered and shaved every part of herself, and then she'd expertly done her hair and makeup. She'd even applied some color to Ashlee's nipples and labia. That had been awkward. And a little arousing.

Now Ashlee was naked except for black, thigh high stockings and a garter belt to hold them up. Mila had told her to kneel on the bed while she locked a spreader bar between her ankles that held her legs open wide.

At Mila's direction, Ashlee had bent forward, laying her chest flat on the bed and reaching each arm out toward the corners. Mila had restrained her in that position with leather cuffs on her wrists that she chained to the corners of the headboard.

Ashlee had never felt so vulnerable. There was no way for her to move, and her ass was up in the air like an open invitation. With her legs forced apart, John would have easy access to whatever part of her he wanted to use.

If he came.

"Oh don't worry, honey," Mila had laughed when Ashlee expressed her worry. "He'll *come.*"

Mila had laid out a variety of scary looking tools on the bed next to Ashlee. A long, hard wooden paddle with holes punched through it. An innocent looking cane that Mila told her had caused most of her welts and that made a distressing whistling sound when she slashed it through the air to demonstrate. A leather whip-like thing that had knotted strands hanging from a well worn handle. And a little silver object that Ashlee had to ask about.

"Do you like anal sex, Ashlee?" Mila had responded.

"Um, n-no. I mean, we've never--"

"Okay, then this might be a bit of a stretch."

Mila picked up the metal thing and knelt behind Ashlee. Ashlee's heart started to race, and she realized that Mila could do *anything* to her. She barely knew the woman, and she'd just invited her into her home and allowed her to fully restrain her in a sexually submissive position on her own bed.

Ashlee tried to calm herself down, but it was no use. Being so vulnerable suddenly filled her with fear. Then Mila's soft hands were suddenly touching her, and to her shame she felt her pussy gush with a wet heat that was surely obvious to the other woman.

Mila fingers were slippery with some kind of lubrication, and she was rubbing firmly against Ashlee's tightly puckered ass hole.

"Ready?"

"For-for what?"

Mila just laughed, and then her fingers were replaced with a cold, firm pressure. Oh God! Ashlee realized that whatever the little silver thing was -- *not so little!* -- Mila was forcing it into her anus.

Ashlee groaned. It was horrible, but she had no choice. Suddenly she remembered what Mila had said back in her kitchen. *I don't like the feeling in the moment that it's happening, but I love being dominated...*

Ashlee was shaking and uncomfortable, but she realized to her shock that was also so turned on that she almost couldn't stand it. The butt plug was fully inserted now, and the painful stretch was starting to ease as her body adjusted to accommodate it.

Mila grabbed Ashlee's phone from the nightstand and scrolled through her contacts until she found John's number. She opened a new text screen and started snapping pictures of Ashlee from different angles, then typed a few words and hit send.

"I'm sure he'll be here before long," Mila said confidently. "So I'm going to go."

Ashlee just nodded. It was all or nothing, now. All she could do was wait and see if her husband would accept what she was offering, and if it would be enough to save her marriage.

As she listened to the sound of Mila leaving and locking up behind her, Ashlee hoped so. She'd always been willing to obey John in their marriage, hadn't she vowed to do just that when she'd said "I do"? She just hadn't known how far she would need to take it.

Now that Mila had shown her the way, it made total sense. She needed to prove to both of them that she could give herself to him completely in order for them to move forward with the kind of marriage they both craved.

Ashlee's shoulders were starting to ache, but she'd been so lost in her thoughts that she hadn't really noticed. The sound of the front door opening jolted her back to the present. Her heart started racing and she licked her lips nervously. John's heavy footsteps sounded on the stairs and then the bedroom door swung open.

"Ashlee?"

CHAPTER FOUR

John still couldn't believe the pictures his wife had sent to his phone. It had started beeping repeatedly in the middle of a sales meeting, and he'd grimaced as he realized that he'd forgotten to turn it to vibrate.

He hadn't been on top of his game for months now, ever since he'd started having troubles with Ashlee. He didn't understand what had gone wrong between them. She'd been compliant and willing when they'd met, and the first year of their marriage had been perfect. Lately, though, she seemed to balk at everything he told her to do.

Aiden had pulled him aside after the meeting, just as John was scrolling through his messages. *Holy shit!* At first he hadn't realized the pictures were of Ashlee. His *wife.* Ashlee, bound to their bed. Ashlee, spread and ready for him. Ashlee, submissive and waiting.

John had to adjust his cock.

"Everything okay?" Aiden asked innocently as John tucked his phone away.

"Uh, something's come up at home."

"Why don't you head out and take care of it," Aiden said with a wink.

John didn't stop to wonder why his hard ass boss was suddenly so accomodating. He didn't stop to wonder anything, like -- who had taken those pictures if his wife was chained to the bed? He just raced for his car.

John kept glancing at the pictures as he drove home. It was a wonder he made it there safely, especially since he let himself stroke his cock a few times on the way. All thoughts of the divorce paperwork he'd served her with were forgotten as he took the stairs two at a time and burst into their bedroom.

"Ashlee?"

Even after getting the pictures, he could hardly believe it. After the mad rush to get there he hesitated, then walked toward her slowly. A part of him was worried that the vision in front of him might disappear if he moved too fast.

"What's going on?" he asked thickly as he ran a hand down her quivering flank.

"That's up to you."

John noticed the silver plug in Ashlee's ass and sucked in a breath. Unzipping himself with one hand, he ran a finger over the protruding end. Her little whimper at the pressure made him even harder.

"Do you want me to fuck you, Ash?"

"Always."

He took a minute to strip completely while his eyes roamed over her restrained body hungrily. She was chained in the middle of the bed, so John had to climb up and kneel behind her to get in position.

He'd always loved Ashlee's shape, with her tight, round ass, firm breasts, and smooth skin. Seeing her bound and presented for his pleasure took his appreciation to a whole new level. Suddenly he could imagine using her harder than he ever had before, and far rougher than their usual lovemaking.

As he climbed up behind he, cock jutting in front of him, he couldn't pull his eyes away from the silver plug pointing at him like a target. He'd never sodomized anyone before, but suddenly taking her that way was all he could think about.

Then he noticed that she'd shaved everything. Seeing her raw and fully exposed inflamed him even further, and he lined his shaft up with her slick cunt. Her ass would have to wait.

"Who sent the pictures?"

"Mila."

John gasped and drove his cock into her. *Mila.* His boss's wife, who let him do *anything* to her. When Ashlee accused him of comparing her to Mila, it was true. The fantasy of having full access to anything he wanted, whenever he wanted, with a woman who wouldn't -- *couldn't* -- say no had been building within him for months.

And now it was coming true.

Ashlee tensed and cried out as he buried himself to the hilt inside her. She'd been slick, but not fully ready for him. His brutal thrust had forced her open in a way that was more satisfying than anything he'd felt before. And she felt *tight.* The plug taking up room in her ass was forcing her wet channel to squeeze his cock even more than usual. It was fucking fantastic!

John groaned and pulled himself almost all the way out, and then slammed into her again. He'd fantasized about different ways he could use his wife on the whole drive over, but now that he was actually fucking her he couldn't seem to stop. He pounded into her like a jack-hammer, feeling his own balls tighten with a rising urgency that he couldn't stop.

"Fuck!"

John came with a brutal rush that left him light headed, and he let himself sag against her sweating body as he realized that he hadn't thought even once about his wife's pleasure.

He *always* waited for her, usually forcing her to come once or twice before he let himself go. But this time was different. She had been just a vessel for his pleasure, and the force of his orgasm had been almost frightening.

CHAPTER FIVE

Ashlee was shaking. Her husband had barely said two words to her before climbing onto the bed and fucking her like a dirty slut. And she'd loved it.

He'd pulled out after he came and she could hear him, excited and still breathing heavily behind her. His warm cum had started to leak out of her, and her pussy felt bruised and sore from the pounding she'd taken.

She couldn't see what John was doing. She felt the bed shift, and then without warning her ass was streaked with fire. Ashlee cried out and tried to jerk away, but she was too tightly restrained.

"John!" she gasped.

She heard a whistling through the air again as he swung the cat o'nine against her burning flesh. This time, some of the knotted leather straps licked at her aching pussy. Tears started leaking from her eyes as she gasped at the burning pain. She clenched in anticipation and the silver plug inside her send shivers of sensation down to her throbbing cunt.

Her husband didn't answer, just continued to whip her as his own breathing became more erratic. Ashlee had never been hit in any way before, and to be bound and helpless and have to take it from the man she loved was as humbling as it was painful. Before long she was sobbing, and her lower body was wracked with waves of hot agony.

"You've disobeyed me, Ash," John ground out as he flogged her.

"I-I'm sorry."

"You vowed to give me your body and your heart in marriage, but you betrayed your vows."

"No! I--"

Thwack.

"*Don't* argue, Ashlee."

"Yes, sir."

"Do you still want to be mine?"

"Yes."

"Completely?"

"Yes!"

He brought the brutal leather down on her one last time and then climbed up behind her. She couldn't see him, but she could tell by the sounds he was making how much punishing her had excited him.

The pain was cleansing, washing away any resistance and reminding her of how loved she always felt when John took charge of her. Without any warning, he pulled the plug out of ass and pressed his cock against her untried back entrance.

"I'm going to fuck you in the ass now, and I want to hear you thank me."

He squirted the lube Mila had left for him onto her hole to ease his way. The little toy had stretched her open enough that he could squeeze the head of his cock in without too much resistance, but her dark channel was tight and untried and resisted his forward advance.

Ashlee felt like she was being ripped in two. John's cock was much thicker than the plug Mila had forced into her, and she gasped as he gripped her burning red cheeks for leverage and pushed his way into her.

"Say thank you," John ordered as he pulled back and plunged in even deeper.

"Th-thank you, baby," she groaned.

He continued to force his way further into her with short, hard thrusts. She could feel herself opening for him, and the painful stretching mingled with the rough friction as he fucked her made her wish she could reach down and rub her clit.

"Please, John," she panted. "More."

He growled and drove himself in again. And again. He'd finally managed to sheath his full length in her ass, and he attacked it with the same ferocity that he'd fucked her pussy with when he arrived.

Ashlee moaned and cried out under the pounding onslaught, feeling her body tighten around him as he drove her closer to her own peak.

"Fuck me harder, baby, *please.*"

John spanked her welt covered ass with his bare hand as he hammered his cock into her dirty hole. Even bound and restrained, she was thrashing against him, begging for more. And he gave it to her, fucking her hard and fast until she came with a piercing scream that made him come, too.

Panting, John rolled off of his wife and lay on the bed next to her. He looked over at her tear streaked face.

"I want you to stay like this tonight."

"Chained to the bed?"

"Yes."

"Are you going to use me again?"

"Yes."

Ashlee was aching and sore and covered in cum. Her husband had fucked her hard and without any consideration, and he was telling her that it wasn't over. She pulled against her restraints as he stood up to examine the other spanking implements Mila had left for them and turned her head away from John to hide her smile.

She couldn't wait.

CLAIRE DISOBEYS

A DOMESTIC DISCIPLINE SPANKING
ROMANCE

CHAPTER ONE

Claire flinched and jerked her hips away from her husband's hard cock. No matter how many times they tried it, the minute she felt his thick head touch her sensitive, puckered anus she found herself pulling away.

"I'm sorry," she cried. "Greg, honey, I just can't."

Rubbing her curvy ass, Greg hushed her and leaned forward to kiss the back of her neck tenderly. The position wedged his throbbing erection between her ass cheeks, which only made her cry harder. She knew how badly he wanted to take her that way, but so far she hadn't been able to make herself do it.

"Don't worry about it, baby," Greg reassured her as he straightened up behind her. "You tried, and that's all that matters."

Tears leaked out of Claire's eyes as her husband rubbed himself against her. She knew she was failing him, but she just couldn't seem to do anything about it. And this was one time that she knew he was wrong. Trying was *not* all that mattered. She had to find a way to give him what he really wanted.

As Greg pulled back and repositioned his cock at the wet entrance of her pussy, Claire resolved to do better. Whatever it takes, she told herself, and then gave up thinking as her husband thrust into her.

Oh, *God*. Greg had a long, thick cock that never failed to satisfy her. He had made them wait until they were married to sleep together, and when she'd first seen the size of him on her wedding night it had made her nervous. Claire didn't come to Greg a virgin, but her sexual experience before him had been extremely limited. And nothing that had prepared her for her husband's massive tool.

She needn't have worried. Greg was always gentle and respectful, treating her like a cherished, china doll when she was good and disciplining her firmly and thoroughly when she was not. In the beginning, he'd actually been more careful with her in the bedroom than she needed. Once she got used to his size and realized how good it felt, she'd had to beg and plead with him to believe her when she told him that she wanted *more*, harder, rougher, and faster.

His giant cock felt amazing, and once he'd finally realized that she meant it he'd happily fucked her the way she wanted. Claire was such a perfect, submissive wife outside the bedroom that Greg had been truly shocked when he'd realized how much she liked hard fucking, but he was more than happy to oblige.

They'd only been married for a few months, and a few weeks ago he'd admitted to her how much he wanted to fuck her in the ass. The thought terrified her. As much as she enjoyed his size inside her, Claire had never been sodomized, and she was sure that if they tried he'd rip her open.

Regardless, she knew that it was her duty as his wife to comply with anything he wanted. Claire and Greg practiced Domestic Discipline, a lifestyle where they both acknowledged that Greg was in charge as the Head of Household, and it was Claire's role to accept his authority in all things.

She trusted that he knew best, and readily submitted to his discipline and punishment when she broke the rules or forgot her place. Except in this. He was so good to her, so patient, that the fact the she hadn't yet let him have what he wanted made her feel horrible.

Even though Greg always insisted it was fine, Claire *knew* how much he wanted to try anal sex. Just the mention of it made him as hard as steel, and even though she hadn't been able to bring herself to let him, he'd been fucking her doggystyle more and more lately, stroking and fingering her puckering hole while he groaned behind her.

Greg would never say it, but Claire knew she was failing him as a wife. In the end it didn't matter if she was nervous or not, she had vowed to love, honor, and obey him and she wasn't living up to those vows. Her sweet husband never complained, but Claire was determined to find a way to give him what he wanted.

CHAPTER TWO

Claire glanced at the clock and then snapped the handcuffs closed with a determined *click*. Immediately, her heart started to pound and she gave an involuntary little cry. Tugging her wrists against the cold metal, she started to feel panicked at the finality of her decision. The cuffs were tight, and her frantic motion was only hurting her. Forcing herself to relax, she stretched out on the bed. There was no going back now.

In the week since their last attempt at anal sex, Claire had given a lot of thought to what it would take for her to get over her fear and give Greg what he wanted. What she *owed* him as his wife. What he deserved as her husband.

She'd finally realized that she was thinking about it backwards. She didn't need to get over her fear -- that seemed virtually impossible -- she just had to find a way to stop herself from pulling away from him. And to convince him that it was his right, and that he should use her the way he needed to instead of catering to her whimpering cowardice.

As much as it went against her nature, Claire had decided to take matters into her own hands. She had bought the handcuffs online and hidden the key so that Greg couldn't find it when he got home. She only hoped that she would be brave enough not to tell him where they were until he was done with her.

Greg was due home any minute and Claire had done everything she could to prepare herself for him. That morning she'd gotten waxed, and her entire body -- including the parts of her that would be most exposed -- was now smooth and hairless. She'd carefully cleaned herself inside and out, and even bought some sexual lubricant, blushing furiously the entire time.

Just before she'd locked herself up, Claire had left Greg a vague but urgent message asking him to hurry home. At that point she'd still wondered if she had the courage to go through with it. If she didn't, she could always come up with some reason for her odd text. Instead of backing out, though, she told herself not to think, just to act.

She'd come up to the bedroom and stripped off her clothes. Laying the little tube on the bedcover where he would have an easy time reaching it, she'd laid herself out, carefully threading the handcuffs through an opening in their headboard. Not letting herself pause to think, she'd clicked the cuff closed on her left wrist, and then, awkwardly and with finality, she'd closed it around her right wrist.

She was now naked and exposed, lying on her stomach with her arms over her head and her wrists crossed. There was no way she could get out of this position until she told her husband where the key was. She knew she'd cut it close, but she'd wanted it that way. She'd only left herself about ten minutes before the time Greg was supposed to be home. It wasn't long, but the time seemed to stretch out agonizingly slowly as she waited, fully exposed and vulnerable, for her husband to arrive.

Claire heard her cell phone buzz a couple of times with Greg's customized text message tone, but of course she couldn't reach it. She smiled, hoping that the fact that she wasn't answering would inspire him to hurry faster. Not, of course, that she wanted to worry him, but she *did* want to get this over with as quickly as possible -- both to satisfy Greg and to prove to herself that she could do it.

Finally, she heard the front door open.

"Claire!" Greg called out urgently from downstairs.

"I'm in the bedroom," she called back, her voice trembling slightly.

Claire turned her head so that she had a good view of the door when Greg came rushing in. He skidded to a halt just inside the room, the look on his face equal parts shock, lust, and anger.

"What the hell?" he finally sputtered. "Baby, what-- Are you *handcuffed?*"

Claire swallowed convulsively. The lust and shock she'd expected, but the fact that he also looked pissed made her want to shrivel up and cower away from him. But she couldn't. Silently, she nodded.

"I don't know what you think you're doing, but give me the key and let's get you out of there," Greg said sternly as he walked toward her.

"N-no, honey," Claire managed to squeak out past the lump in her throat. "It's time for you to get what you've always wanted. You know I haven't been able to give it to you, and this is the only way I could think of to do my duty."

"Claire, this is crazy. Tell me where the key is," Greg ordered.

He was standing next to the bed now, and even though his words were saying no he couldn't stop himself from running a hand down her naked body. Claire was so used to obeying him that she almost gave in, but then she noticed the bulge in his pants.

"No," she repeated more firmly. "Greg, this is your chance. I want you to fuck me in the ass."

"Are you defying me?" he asked incredulously, even as he kept touching her.

Trembling, Claire nodded.

"On your knees," he commanded her.

Claire did as she was told, awkwardly raising herself up and trying to prepare herself to take his huge cock in her ass. To her surprise, instead of pulling out his straining erection, Greg scowled at her and stalked over to the closet.

Oh, God. That could only mean one thing. He wasn't going to fuck her. He was going to punish her for her disobedience.

Squeezing her eyes closed, Claire tried to brace herself for what was coming. Usually, when Greg disciplined her, he warmed her up with his hand before pulling out any of the stronger spanking tools. Today, though, he didn't show her that mercy.

Without warning, the hard wooden paddle that she hated cracked against the tops of her thighs and drove her forward onto her face.

"Get back up," Greg ordered in a voice thick with lust.

Claire did. He cracked the paddle into her again, raining stinging fire down on her sensitive buttocks. Claire cried out, but managed to stay up on her knees this time. Breathing hard, her husband continued to punish her with stinging blows that reddened her skin and made her entire lower body feel like it was on fire.

Claire was a good girl, and Greg rarely had to discipline or punish her. When he did, it had always been over his knee. This was different. Claire had never felt as exposed and vulnerable as she did now, and with each crack of the paddle she sobbed harder.

Finally, it was over.

"Spread your knees."

The paddle landed on the carpet with a muffled thump, and Claire felt the bed dip as he leaned a knee on it. His hot hands caressed her ass, kneading and massaging the reddened flesh before pulling her cheeks apart for a long moment.

"What-- what are you doing?" she finally asked.

"Baby," he answered softly. "You must never disobey me. Even when you mean well."

"I know," she whispered. "I'm sorry."

She felt his thumbs start to run down the length of her crack, passing over her puckered little hole and causing her to shiver.

"Every time I spank you, I see *this*," he told her, pressing against the sensitive little star and making her gasp. "It calls to me, and I've been patient with you up until now."

"You don't need to be," Claire interrupted. "That's why I'm doing this. Honey, I'm *yours*."

Letting out a shuddering breath, Greg backed off the bed and stood up. Claire twisted around to look at him and got a hard smack on her ass for her trouble.

"Stay still," he ordered urgently.

He was stripping off his clothes, and with a sudden rush of adrenaline Claire realized that he was really going to do it. He'd punished her for her disobedience, but he was still going to take what she was offering. She was both thrilled and terrified, and she trembled on the bed while she waited for him to use her the way he'd been aching to.

Finally, he climbed back onto the bed, naked, kneeling behind her. He cupped her ass and she shivered. Her pussy started to tingle at his nearness, but knowing what was coming also made her stomach tighten in fear. He was so big, she didn't know if she'd be able to take his cock in her ass.

He ran his hand down the back of her thighs, spreading her legs apart even wider. Claire knew she was fully exposed to him now, and she knew it excited him.

"I-I bought some lubricant, honey," she whispered.

She heard the soft shush of his hand on the bedspread as he picked up the little tube. A moment later, he'd lubed his fingers and pressed one slick, thick digit against her anus. Claire gasped, and tried to jerk away. The hard metal digging into her wrists reminded her that this time, she couldn't.

Greg started rubbing his finger firmly over her hole in little circles. Claire couldn't stop shaking, but this she time forced herself to hold still.

"Try to relax, honey," he urged her, then pushed the thick digit inside her. Clair had to suck in her breath as she butt clenched spasmodically around the sudden intrusion. It was uncomfortable and awkward, but despite that, Claire felt proud of herself. In all their anal play before Greg had never gotten this far.

He started to thrust his finger in and out of her slowly, and she gasped in surprise. To her shock, despite a little bit of pain, it was starting to arouse her. Without thinking she pressed herself back toward him, forcing his finger in even deeper.

"That's right, baby," Greg groaned, and then forced a second finger inside her. Claire moaned.

"You like that?" he growled.

"I - I don't know," she whispered. Then, "Yes. Greg, please, I want you to fuck me. Fuck me in the ass."

Her words obviously excited him, and he started scissoring his fingers inside her, forcing her to loosen up. It was too much, too fast, and Claire started to tighten up again. Without a word, Greg spanked her, hard, and she forced herself to relax as he pushed a third finger into her from behind.

"Stop resisting," he ordered. "You're the one who reminded me that you're here to do as I say. And right now, I'm going to give you what you just asked for."

Squirming against his hand, Claire felt a hot rush of wetness between her legs. He was right, and suddenly the thought excited her. Tugging against the cuffs, she realized that she had no choice but to give in and take it. She had nowhere to go, but suddenly she didn't want to be anywhere but here.

She had been so scared of taking his cock in her ass that it shocked her to realize that the feeling of his fingers buried inside her was exciting her. That she was actually getting impatient for more.

"Please, honey," she panted. "Do it!"

Greg didn't need any further encouragement. Pulling his fingers, out he squirted some extra lube on his huge cock and then lined it up with her untried backhole. Slowly, he started to push his way in.

Claire trembled as her body stretched to accommodate his thickness. She felt her skin start to glow with a light sweat as she shuddered and panted beneath him. He held her tightly by the hips as he inched inside the vise-like grip of her back channel.

"Oh, *God*," he groaned behind her. "You're so tight back here, Claire. So fucking *hot.*"

The excitement in his voice turned her on more than she expected. He'd only managed to push in a few inches, and she whimpered a little as he pulled himself back out. With another deep groan, he drove himself forward again more forcefully.

This time he got a little bit further in, and Claire welcomed the painful stretching as the friction started to excite her even more. Her body wouldn't stop shaking as Greg pulled back and thrust forward, again and again, each time gaining a little more depth until, at last, he was able to bury himself completely.

"Oh, fuck, Claire," he ground out, his voice shaking. "I don't know if I can last. My cock is splitting you open."

"Are you looking at it?" she gasped, the image making her moan with excitement.

Greg pulled himself back until just the head of his cock was still inside her, then slammed all the way in with a groan. And then he did it again.

"*Yes,*" he finally answered as he started to fuck her harder. "I love seeing it disappear inside you. Jesus, Claire!"

He suddenly reached underneath her and roughly rubbed his fingers against her clit. Claire cried out at the sudden stimulation, and then started begging for more as he continued to fuck and rub her faster and faster.

"Baby, you've got to come *now*," he ordered.

With a sharp cry, she obeyed. As her body pulsed in shuddering waves around his massive cock, he let loose with his own shout and filled her ass with hot, hot cum.

With a breathless laugh, Greg collapsed on top of her once they both stopped shaking. Claire had almost forgotten she was cuffed, but his weight flattened her on the bed and made her wrists jerk against the steel rings, reminding her. His softening cock was still buried deep in her ass, and she didn't want to move.

"You do know where the key is, don't you, baby?" he finally whispered in her ear.

"Mm-hmm," she replied with a little shiver as he started kissing her neck. "It's--"

"Wait!" Greg cut her off. "Don't tell me yet."

Claire sucked in a breath as she felt him start to swell again inside her. Greg started gently rocking against her, reaching under her to palm her full breasts and tweak her nipples roughly.

"That's right, baby," he praised her as she squirmed under him with rising excitement. "You're not getting loose until I'm done with you."

"Yes, sir," she panted as her husband prepared to fuck her in the ass again.

Burying her face in the bedspread, Claire allowed herself a secret smile as she prepared to enjoy the result of her outrageous disobedience.

AVA'S SUPPLICATION

A DOMESTIC DISCIPLINE SPANKING
ROMANCE

CHAPTER ONE

My parents had freaked out when I told them I was engaged.

"Honey, you're only 18! Give yourself some time to experience life, date different men, find yourself," Mom had begged.

"Your mother is right," Dad had added. Of course. He always agrees with anything Mom says. "And-- Ava, he is, uh, twice your age."

And of course that was their real problem. Bruce is almost as old as my Dad.

We seated them in the front pew at the wedding, and when I promised to "love, honor, and obey" they both winced, looking like they'd just sucked lemons. But I don't care. I love my parents, of course, but it's my life, and I want Bruce.

He got some flack for our relationship, too.

He had been my softball coach in high school. The truth is, we'd never done anything wrong while I was a student. I had definitely fantasized about it though. I actually had my first orgasm masturbating to one of those fantasies, but Bruce was too morally uptight to even look at me before I turned 18.

Well, I guess I shouldn't say he didn't look. I never caught him at it, but after we finally got together he admitted that he'd definitely noticed me. I asked him if he used to pull out his cock while he thought about me, and he wouldn't answer. But I knew he had. I hope he had.

Our softball uniforms had been pretty tight, and I'd looked for any opportunity to make sure he got a good view of my ass. I have a great ass.

I used to find any excuse to bend over in front of him. Sometimes I'd end up with wet panties just from imagining what it would be like if he really did come up behind me and just do it, just fuck me right on the field, in front of everyone. I think he imagined it too, but to this day he's never admitted the details of any of his fantasies about me.

Of course, as soon as we started publicly dating everyone thought it had been going on for years. He ended up losing his job over it, even though no one could ever prove he'd done anything wrong. Because he hadn't.

It's why we moved out of state, and I can't say I'm unhappy about it. Bruce has a great new job lined up, and even though people will be able to tell there's an age gap between us, they won't know our history and we can have a fresh start. Every day, I'm thankful that he loves me enough to have weathered that storm.

Bruce is one of the strongest men I know. Not just his body, which is hot, but the way he's so confident in his own sense of right and wrong. And how he takes charge of every situation.

When he was my coach, the other girls would complain that he was too hard on us, but secretly I loved it. He was the only one in my life who wouldn't sugar coat his opinion, and he never hesitated to correct me. It made me a better player, and a better person.

I admit it, I was spoiled growing up. I'm an only child and my parents showered me with praise and support. I really do appreciate how much they adore me, but Bruce was the first person in my life to tell me the truth when I wasn't good enough. And then help me get better.

My fantasies about Bruce kept me from dating during high school. I just wasn't interested in pimply faced boys when what I wanted was a real man. Bruce was surprised to find me a virgin on our wedding night, but I could tell he really liked it.

It was something else that he didn't like...

CHAPTER TWO

W e were laying in bed when I finally found the courage to bring it up. He had just rolled off me, and I was hoping that after the amazing ride I'd given him he'd be open minded. But that's not really the way it went.

"What?!"

"I really think it's a good fit for us," I told him while I drew little circles on his six-pack with my finger. "And it's not just about the spanking, it-- it's a whole lifestyle. A way for us to have a happier home and build a strong foundation for our marriage."

"I don't care what you call it," he said firmly. "I am not willing to do anything that would hurt you."

I tried to suppress a smile as I noticed that no matter how strong his words were, he couldn't pull away from my hand. He always said he loved my spirit, intelligence, and attitude. But I know for a fact that he could never get enough of my tight teenage body.

"It's called Domestic Discipline. And really all it means is that we both know that you're in charge," I moved my hand down to his sated cock. I'm not above using whatever I have to to get what I want.

"I'm not going to punish you, baby," he told me in a strained voice as I started to stroke him to hardness. "I married you because I want a wife, not a child."

"Does that mean I don't get to call you 'Daddy'?" I asked cheekily before bending over him and taking his cock in my mouth.

"Avaaaaaaaaaa," he groaned.

I loved sucking his cock. I'd fantasized about it for years, and the first time he'd turned down my advances -- *"No sex before marriage, Ava"* -- I'd dropped to my knees and had him unzipped before he knew what hit him.

He couldn't resist then, and it was no different now. As I rolled my tongue around his sensitive head and sucked him into the back of my throat I felt his hands fist in my hair. I smiled around his thick shaft.

Bobbing over him, I used my hand to stroke the length that I couldn't get in my mouth. I fondled his balls and felt them start to tighten as I brought him closer and closer to happiness.

He usually pulled me off of him before he came and insisted on returning the favor, or at least fucking me so I got to come, too. But this time, I didn't let him.

I clamped my lips around him and did my best to turn my mouth into a vacuum cleaner. Sucking him hard and deep, I refused to stop until he exploded. Finally, his hips thrust up and slammed into my face, and with a shout he spurted hot, salty cum into my mouth. Struggling to swallow all of his seed, I finally let him go and lay back next to him, wiping my chin and laughing.

"I am most definitely not your child, *Daddy*," I teased.

"Don't call me that!" he said with a growl. "And-- you know I like to make you happy, baby, but I really don't think I could stand making you cry with this spanking idea. Please don't ask me to punish you."

Rolling on top of him, I laid my petite naked body on his and looked seriously into his eyes.

"This is important to me, Bruce," I said. "Ever since I met you, you've been my guiding light. You're the only one who ever held me accountable. Who cared enough to call me out when needed, and give me consequences that helped me become better.

This is no different. It's just that instead of making me run laps, you'll bend me over your knee whenever needed and take your bare hand to my little round ass…"

I was starting to get turned on. I ground my tingling pussy against him and knew I had won when he flipped me over and started kissing me like a starving man. I grinned in anticipation. His skill in the bedroom was most definitely one of the things I loved about being married to an older man.

CHAPTER THREE

Bruce had me in tears.

I was finding that it was one thing to want him to be the Head of Household, and quite another to live it. Don't get me wrong, in the weeks since he'd finally agreed to try Domestic Discipline we had both loved the changes it brought to our marriage.

Knowing he was in charge made me feel loved and protected in a way I'd never experienced before. His absolute authority in our lives gave me a freedom and peace I'd been craving without even knowing it.

Just as he had when he was my coach, he held me accountable and corrected me when I strayed from the rules he set for our marriage. We both noticed how much less chaotic day to day living felt, and just as I'd hoped, it provided a solid structure as we built our lives together.

Crack!

I tried to remind myself of all of this as he brought a wooden paddle down on my fiery red ass again. When Bruce agreed to do something, he made sure to do it right. My curvy little backside had been as red as a cherry for most of the week, as he worked hard to help me correct my bad habits.

I was completely naked in the middle of the living room. My husband had ordered me to bend over and hold my ankles, and was halfway through the punishment he'd promised me that morning when I overdrew our checking account again.

The spanking was definitely working. I'd already managed to stop some pretty ingrained bad habits. But *fuck!* It hurt!

He was breathing heavily behind me when he finally stopped. He didn't hold back, and I knew it was a bit of a workout for him when he properly spanked me. But I also knew that having to stare at my little shaved pussy winking out at him while he reddened my ass got him excited.

"Get down on your hands and knees," he ordered me thickly as he tossed the paddle aside.

I did as I was told, and, despite the throbbing ache in my lower body, my cunt clenched tight. I really, really hoped he was about to fuck me.

Spanking me had done wonders for our marriage in more ways than I'd expected. Getting punished really *did* hold me accountable, but what I hadn't expected was the effect it would have on my straight-laced husband.

Before we started DD, Bruce treated me a bit like a china doll. He loved fucking me, but he always did it a bit carefully. Not only was he older than me, but he was a *lot* bigger and stronger than me. I think he used to try really hard to make sure I didn't feel overpowered by him.

But not anymore. When it came to sex, he had started using me harder and harder, and really exercising his authority over me. He stopped worrying so much about making sure I came every time and just started taking what he needed from me, whenever he wanted.

I loved it.

As soon as I was down on all fours he kneeled behind me and pulled my knees apart even wider. Putting one hand between my shoulder blades, he forced my chest down to the ground and held it there while he fit his thick cock into my little slit.

He didn't bother to check if I was ready, which just made me wetter. Driving himself in to the hilt with one thrust, he started pounding into me from behind while he held me down with his other hand.

"God, baby, you are so hot," he ground out.

I knew he was staring at the welts he'd left on my ass. He couldn't keep his hands off of it, stroking and slapping it while he fucked me. Seeing what he'd wrought drove home the fact that he *owned* me, and I knew it turned him on more than he'd ever expected. I pushed back against him and felt myself tighten with hot lust at the thought.

"I'm going to come, Daddy!" I cried out. He kept telling me not to call him that, but every time I did he got even harder.

With a little sob, I came. My tight teenage sheath milked his cock, and he almost lost it. Breathing hard, he pulled his rock hard shaft out of me and started rubbing it up and down my open ass crack.

He was still holding me down, and I lay there breathless, wondering what he would do with me next. I was completely at his mercy. Not just physically, but because I had given him my consent to use me as he needed.

"I'm yours," I'd told him when he had finally agreed to do this. "I will submit to your authority in every way."

"Shoot, Ava," he'd laughed and looked away. My big, strong husband actually blushed. "We are talking about a *marriage*, here, not about making you my sex slave."

The sex slave comment totally turned me on.

"I'm talking about what I'm willing-- what I *want*, to do for you, Daddy," I'd said with a pout. He frowned at that word of course, but I could see his cock twitch.

"You care for and protect me, and I'm here to take the stress off of you so that you can focus on leading our household. That means more than just me doing laundry and dishes. It means that anytime I can help you relax by making you come..."

I had started stroking him through his pants. He knew I was right.

"Look, all I'm saying is, take whatever you need from me. I just want you to know that I'm already agreeing to it, so you don't need to ask. Use me however you want. Whatever, whenever, don't hold back."

Bruce had finally started taking me at my word, and I loved the way he'd stopped asking permission when it came to my body. In just a few weeks he'd gotten used to holding me down or spreading my legs if that's what he wanted, forcing me to my knees and shoving his cock in my mouth whenever he needed, or just bending me over when he got home and fucking me raw.

But there were still some ways he'd never used me.

"Stay down," he ordered me now as he removed his hand from my shoulders. He grabbed the rounded mounds of my ass cheeks and spread them wide. I felt his thick thumb slide down the length of my crack and circle my clenched little star.

Instantly, a bolt of electric heat shot to my clit. He continued to rub my back hole firmly, and after a minute he forced his thumb inside.

I moaned, and arched my back to push against the intrusion. I was an anal virgin, and if I had to guess I'd say Bruce had never gone there before, either. But now that he had, I wanted more.

Rocking slightly back and forth, I helped him ease his way into my tight ass. Pretty soon, he was circling his thumb inside me, and he reached underneath with his other hand and rubbed my clit.

"Oh my God!" I screamed. "Daddy, please fuck me in the ass!"

"Ava," he panted. I knew he wanted to.

He started pumping his thumb in and out of me, and I knew I was going to come again. But before I could, he pulled it out and replaced it with two fingers. It was a painful stretch, and I sucked in a breath as I tried to get used to it.

He wasn't waiting for me. Before I knew what was happening, he'd shoved a third finger into my ass and I whimpered and tried to pull away. I was pretty small anyway, and three of his thick, callused fingers really hurt.

Smack! He cracked his bare hand down on my sore ass, *hard*.

"Don't move," he ordered in a tense voice. "You're going to take whatever I give you, and in a minute, that's going to be my cock."

I moaned desperately. It still hurt, but nothing made me hornier than having him take command. I didn't care what it felt like, I wanted him to *do it*.

As if he read my mind, he pulled his fingers out and pushed the tip of his cock against my anus. It had immediately closed up when his fingers came out, but he pushed forward relentlessly until the thick mushroom head of his rock hard erection was fully inside me.

His cock was much thicker than the three fingers he'd used, and I panted hard as I tried to relax and take it. As soon as he got his head in, he grabbed onto my hips and drove himself all the way into my back channel with one thrust.

"Fucccckkkkk!!!" I screamed as he forced me open.

Bruce didn't even pause. Holding me in an iron grip, he jackhammered my tight ass like a madman.

"Call me Daddy!" he ordered.

"Yes, Daddy! Fuck me, Daddy!" I panted.

"You love my cock in every hole, don't you," he ground out.

"I love your cock, Daddy! My ass loves your cock! I want your cum dripping out of my ass *every day!*"

With a sharp hiss, he slammed into me one more time and gave me what I'd asked for. I felt his cock throbbing as he released his load, and I couldn't stand it.

Breaking his "don't move" rule, I shoved my hand down to my pussy and frantically rubbed my clit. I wanted to come before he pulled out of my ass, and when he saw what I was doing he spanked me, hard.

That did it. With a shout, my orgasm roared through me like a tidal wave. Bruce waited until he felt the ripples end, and then pulled himself out. Gathering me into his arms, he kissed me.

"You did great, baby," he said approvingly.

I snuggled closer to my husband, smiling in contentment as his cum leaked out of my stretched hole. My ass was throbbing from the spanking and the fucking, and I couldn't help wondering if he'd remember that I'd disobeyed him when I moved my hand at the end. I knew I needed to be punished for that.

Sighing in contentment, I made a mental note to bring it up later in case he forgot.

Be the first to find out about all of Lee Riley's new releases, book sales, and freebies by joining her VIP Mailing List. Join today and get a FREE book -- instantly!

Check Lee Riley's website spicybestsellers.com for more books.

ABOUT LEE RILEY

Lee Riley is an adventurous writer who creates spicy short stories that challenge conventions and leave readers on the edge of their seats. Drawing inspiration from their travels, Lee explores the world with insatiable curiosity, using these experiences to craft stories that captivate readers.

When not writing, Lee indulges their passion for the outdoors, discovering new culinary delights, and making connections with people from all walks of life. Their love for adventure and zest for life is reflected in their work, which is daring, unconventional, and full of surprises.

More on www.spicybestsellers.com

Contact me at lee@spicybestsellers.com